www.enchantedlion.com

First English-language edition published in 2021 by Enchanted Lion Books
248 Creamer Street, Suite 4, Brooklyn, NY 11231
Original Korean-language edition copyright © 2017 by Woongjin Thinkbig
Text copyright © 2017 by Lee Juck
Illustrations copyright © 2017 by Kim Seung-youn
English-language translation copyright © 2021 by Enchanted Lion Books
Editors, English-language text: Claudia Bedrick, Emilie Robert Wong, and Aubrey Nolan
All rights reserved
All rights reserved under International and Pan-American Copyright Conventions
A CIP is on record with the Library of Congress
ISBN 978-1-59270-313-5
Printed in Italy by Società Editoriale Grafiche AZ

First Printing

One Day

Written by Lee Juck

Illustrated by Kim Seung-youn

Translated from Korean by
Asuka Minamoto, Lee Juck, and Dianne Chung

Enchanted Lion Books
NEW YORK

One day,

Grandpa is gone.

Clothing Donation Bin

Grandpa is gone.

His shoes sit in the closet,
waiting to be worn.

Grandpa is gone.

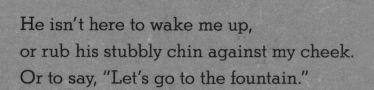

He isn't here to wake me up,
or rub his stubbly chin against my cheek.
Or to say, "Let's go to the fountain."

Grandpa is gone.

Grandma keeps rubbing my back.
She won't stop giving me food.
I eat everything without complaining.
If I didn't, I think she would cry.

Grandpa is gone.

The man from the stationery store
drops off Grandpa's name stamp.
He asks why Grandpa hasn't picked it up.
Dad gets a newspaper to try it out.
Soon, Grandpa's name covers the page.

At the fountain, everybody asks about Grandpa.

Why did Grandpa leave without telling his friends?
I mean, he always tapped me on the head
when I didn't say a proper goodbye.

Grandpa is gone.

As hard as I look, I can't find him anywhere.

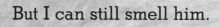

asa

But I can still smell him.

I wrap myself up in his jacket
and spend all day
breathing in Grandpa's scent.

It's pitch black when I wake up.
I guess I fell asleep.

Grandpa is gone.

He must have come from someplace far, far away.
A place across the universe, full of dazzling stars.

Note: The term "Nasa" refers to wool, or a woolen fabric mixed with other materials, such as cotton or silk. The term was commonly used in the names of stores that sold men's suits after the 1950s.

To see a video about
this book, check out
our Vimeo channel:
https://vimeo.com/
enchantedlion